Prissy & Pop

Big Day Out

This book is dedicated to
the students at the Bolles School

Special thanks to my parents for their love and support, P and P Designs for Prissy's precious bows,
Woofs and Ruffles Couture Dog Clothing for Prissy's bikini, and Grafton Studios.

Prissy and Pop: Big Day Out
Text copyright © 2016 by Melissa Nicholson
Photographs copyright © 2016 by HarperCollins Publishers
For information address HarperCollins Children's Books, a division of
HarperCollins Publishers, 195 Broadway, New York, NY 10007.
www.harpercollinschildrens.com

ISBN 978-0-06-243995-6

Typography by Chelsea C. Donaldson

16 17 18 19 20   SCP   10 9 8 7 6 5 4 3 2 1

First Edition

Prissy&Pop
Big Day Out

By Melissa Nicholson
Photographs by Petra Terova

HARPER
An Imprint of HarperCollinsPublishers

"Wake up, Pop!" says Prissy.

"Rise and shine!"

"But I'm sleepy," Pop cries.

"Silly Pop, c'mon!" says Prissy.

And two little piggies begin a new day.

Prissy knows just what she's going to wear.

But Pop has no idea.

"Ooh! Let's do a fashion show!" Prissy says.

Fabulous!

Classy!

Fetching!

Perfect.

"You look sensational, Pop."

"Thank you, Prissy," says Pop.

These little piggies are always polite.

"What should we have for breakfast?" asks Pop.

"Hmm . . . ," says Prissy, thinking hard. "How about . . . everything!"

"Oh no!" cries Pop. "What a mess."

"Time for a bubble bath," says Prissy.

And two little piggies get cleaned up.

Pop wants to go to the beach.

But Prissy wants to do some gardening first.

Daisies, irises, marigolds—Prissy loves them all.

"Ah-*choo*!" Pop sneezes.

"Gesundheit," says Prissy.

Prissy loves to be polite.

"*Now* is it time for the beach?" Pop asks.

"You bet!" says Prissy.

Pop pulls the car around. "Hop in!"

"Don't mind if I do," says Prissy.

And the two little piggies are off!

Prissy gets hungry on the way to the beach.

"Let's stop for some snacks!"

"And toys!" Pop adds.

So two little piggies go to the market.

"Excellent choices, Pop."

"Thank you, Prissy," says Pop.

"Now just a quick stop at the playground before we hit the waves," Prissy says. Swings, slides, merry-go-rounds—Prissy loves them all.

But Pop is getting impatient.

"A polite piggie would go to the beach RIGHT NOW!"

"You have a point, Silly Pop," says Prissy.

And off they go.

Vroom, vroom, vroom.

"I'm going to build a sand castle," says Pop.

"I'm going to dunk my head," says Prissy.

"I'm going to look for shark teeth!" says Pop.

Sand castles!

Beach snacks!

Surfing!

Sunbathing!

Prissy and Pop love them all.

Two little piggies play in the surf.

Two little piggies dig in the sand.

Two little piggies share their snacks

with each other. . . .

And two little piggies watch the sun go down.

Priscilla's Fun Facts

• I was born all pink but have developed some markings as I have gotten older. I have a spot on my back in the shape of mouse ears and a beauty mark on my snout.

• I have one blue eye and one brown eye.

• I have never tried a food I didn't like. Well . . . except for mushrooms.

• Running on the beach with my mom is one of my favorite activities.

• I jump up when Mom says "snack time" at school, because I know my first-grade friends are going to feed us.

• I love going to Grandma's and getting extra treats.

• I like to play with toys that give out treats.

• I always accessorize with a bow and often pearls.

Poppleton's Fun Facts

- I was not born with the markings around my eye. They developed later and grow with me.

- I have brown eyes.

- Mom says I am a picky eater. I will only eat greens if they are mixed in with yummier foods, like my piggy pellets or carrots.

- Belly rubs are the bee's knees!

- Cover your ears! I squeal if I don't have Mom or Prissy nearby.

- Nothing beats singing with my friends at school.

- I love to root in the sand with my snout. (Rooting is a pig's way of digging.)

- Fences, furniture, and tires are great back scratchers.

Author's Note

Priscilla was born on April 29, 2013. I adopted her that June from Oink Oink Mini Pigs!, having fallen in love with pigs after visiting a pig farm in Alabama while attending college. She was the perfect pink piglet girl I had dreamed of and more. She was a tiny runt at birth, and I could immediately see her spunk and sass from early on. She is truly a little diva princess, and I couldn't imagine her any other way.

After much thought and consideration, I decided to adopt her a companion. Poppleton was born on December 12, 2013, at Island Miniatures. He was also a tiny runt. I adopted him the following March, and our adventures together began. He is the sweetest little piglet and a true mama's boy. He is more laid-back and often very silly, which has earned him the nickname "Silly Pop."

The two have become known as "Prissy and Pop," and they are the best of friends. They snuggle together, follow each other around, and share many adventures. They also accompany me to school each day, where they are class pets in my first-grade room. Prissy and Pop are often integrated into learning activities and teach the students a greater love and respect for animals. The bond the students form with them throughout the year is an experience I think the students will never forget.

Prissy and Pop are very special to me, and I am thrilled that I get to share my love for them with others all over the world. I never dreamed when I started their social media account (at the encouragement of my niece) a few years ago that so many people would fall in love with them. It is always touching to hear how much of a bright spot they are in so many people's days.

Melissa Nicholson

PHOTO

prissy_pig

30,314 likes